W9-AVN-167

Dear Parents and Educators,

Welcome to Penguin Young Readers! As parents and educators, you know that each child develops at his or her own pace—in terms of speech, critical thinking, and, of course, reading. Penguin Young Readers recognizes this fact. As a result, each Penguin Young Readers book is assigned a traditional easy-to-read level (1–4) as well as a Guided Reading Level (A–P). Both of these systems will help you choose the right book for your child. Please refer to the back of each book for specific leveling information. Penguin Young Readers features esteemed authors and illustrators, stories about favorite characters, fascinating nonfiction, and more!

Dog on His Bus

LEVEL **2**

GUIDED
READING
LEVEL **F**

This book is perfect for a **Progressing Reader** who:
- can figure out unknown words by using picture and context clues;
- can recognize beginning, middle, and ending sounds;
- can make and confirm predictions about what will happen in the text; and
- can distinguish between fiction and nonfiction.

Here are some **activities** you can do during and after reading this book:
- Sight Words: Sight words are frequently used words that readers must know just by looking at them. They are known instantly, on sight. Knowing these words helps children develop into efficient readers. As you read the story, have the child point out the sight words below.

a	come	in	the	us
am	I	so	up	with

- Make Connections: The main character in this story is a dog with a job. He is a bus driver! There is also a police dog in the book. Discuss different types of jobs with the child. What does the child want to be when he or she grows up?

Remember, sharing the love of reading with a child is the best gift you can give!

—Bonnie Bader, EdM
  Penguin Young Readers program

*Penguin Young Readers are leveled by independent reviewers applying the standards developed by Irene Fountas and Gay Su Pinnell in *Matching Books to Readers: Using Leveled Books in Guided Reading*, Heinemann, 1999.

Thanks to Renee and Lena—ES

For Emma and Graham—SB

Penguin Young Readers
Published by the Penguin Group
Penguin Group (USA) Inc., 375 Hudson Street, New York, New York 10014, USA
Penguin Group (Canada), 90 Eglinton Avenue East, Suite 700, Toronto, Ontario M4P 2Y3, Canada
(a division of Pearson Penguin Canada Inc.)
Penguin Books Ltd., 80 Strand, London WC2R 0RL, England
Penguin Group Ireland, 25 St. Stephen's Green, Dublin 2, Ireland (a division of Penguin Books Ltd.)
Penguin Group (Australia), 250 Camberwell Road, Camberwell, Victoria 3124, Australia
(a division of Pearson Australia Group Pty. Ltd.)
Penguin Books India Pvt. Ltd., 11 Community Centre, Panchsheel Park, New Delhi—110 017, India
Penguin Group (NZ), 67 Apollo Drive, Rosedale, Auckland 0632, New Zealand
(a division of Pearson New Zealand Ltd.)
Penguin Books (South Africa) (Pty.) Ltd., 24 Sturdee Avenue,
Rosebank, Johannesburg 2196, South Africa

Penguin Books Ltd., Registered Offices: 80 Strand, London WC2R 0RL, England

Text copyright © 2012 by Eric Seltzer. Illustrations copyright © 2012 by Penguin Group (USA) Inc. All rights reserved. Published by Penguin Young Readers, an imprint of Penguin Group (USA) Inc., 345 Hudson Street, New York, New York 10014. Manufactured in China.

Library of Congress Cataloging-in-Publication Data is available.

ISBN 978-0-448-45904-2   10 9 8 7 6 5 4 3 2 1

ALWAYS LEARNING   PEARSON

Dog on His Bus

by Eric Seltzer
illustrated by Sebastien Braun

Penguin Young Readers
An Imprint of Penguin Group (USA) Inc.

I am Dog.

I drive a bus.

I pick up Frog.

Come ride with us.

I drive in rain.

I drive in snow.

I drive in fog.

Off we go.

I make a right

by the lake.

I pick up Hen.

I pick up Snake.

I make a left

by the tree.

I pick up Bug.

I pick up Bee.

Hen and Snake

need a hat.

I drop them off
at Hats by Cat.

Bug and Bee

want a book.

I drop them off,

so they can look.

We pass a cab.

We pass a truck.

Inside the truck

is my friend Duck.

Police Dog waves

hello to me.

I see him every day

at three.

At my next stop,

there is a line.

A line of nine

will fit just fine.

Hungry Bear

wants his lunch.

I drop him off
at Crunch a Bunch.

23

Grandpa Frog

needs a cane.

He gets off

at First and Main.

Oh no.

What now?

My tires blow.

26

I pump them up,

so we can go.

Each day at five,

see what I do.

I park my bus.

I wash it, too.

I love my job.

It is good fun.

I love my bus

and everyone!